Thayer Memorial Library

P.O. Box 5 ✦ 717 Main Street ✦ Lancaster, Massachusetts 01523 ✦ (978)368-8928 ✦ Fax (978)368-8929

ADELE
MUSIC SENSATION

BY JEANNE MARIE FORD

Published by The Child's World®
1980 Lookout Drive • Mankato, MN 56003-1705
800-599-READ • www.childsworld.com

Photographs ©: Dominic Lipinski/Press Association/URN:25623688/AP Images, cover, 1; Featureflash Photo Agency/Shutterstock Images, 5; Robyn Beck/AFP/AP Images, 6; Matt Sayles/AP Images, 8; Helga Esteb/Shutterstock Images, 10; Sandro Campardo/ EPA/Newscom, 12; Ian West/Press Association/URN:12093786/AP Images, 14; Brian J. Ritchie/Hotsauce/Rex Features/AP Images, 16; Shutterstock Images, 18; WAAA/ZDS/ Wenn.com/Newscom, 20

ISBN 9781503819931
LCCN 2016960917

Printed in the United States of America
PA02335

ABOUT THE AUTHOR

Jeanne Marie Ford is an Emmy-winning TV scriptwriter who holds a master of fine arts degree in writing for children from Vermont College. She has written numerous children's books and articles. Ford also teaches college English. She lives in Maryland with her husband and two children.

TABLE OF
CONTENTS

FAST FACTS

Name

- Adele Laurie Blue Adkins

Birthdate

- May 5, 1988

Birthplace

- North London, England

Fun Trivia

- Adele has a pet dachshund named Louie Armstrong. She named him after the famous musician because he howled while listening to Armstrong sing.

- Adele went to high school with fellow hit singer Jessie J. They used to sing together at lunchtime. Another famous **alumna** was singer Amy Winehouse.

- Adele watches at least six to seven movies each week. Her favorite actor is Al Pacino.

- Adele suffers from terrible stage fright. Once she even tried to run away from a concert because she was too scared to go onstage.

- Adele has had only one singing lesson.

Chapter 1

CHASING DREAMS

Adele had always hated dressing up. As she walked the red carpet at the 2009 Grammy Awards, her black cocktail dress was so tight she could barely breathe. Photographers yelled at her to step aside so they could snap photos of better-known **celebrities**.

At her seat, she kicked off her heels and loosened her belt. Then presenter Kanye West said something Adele had not expected: "And the Grammy goes to Adele!"[1]

Stunned, she rushed to the stage barefoot. She had just won the Grammy Award for Best New Artist. "Thank you so much," she finally said. "I'm gonna cry."[2]

◄ **Adele received a Grammy Award for Best New Artist in 2009.**

▲ Adele also won a Grammy Award for Best Female Pop Vocal Performance in 2009.

Adele grew up a world away from the stage in Los Angeles, California. She lived with her mom, Penny, in a poor neighborhood in London, England. Penny turned the bedroom of their **flat** into a performance space. She arranged lamps to form a spotlight. She even sewed Adele a sparkly eye patch to help her imitate her favorite singer, Gabrielle.

Penny filled Adele's childhood with music. She once hid her three-year-old daughter under her coat and snuck her into a concert. One of Adele's favorite early memories was her mother's gift of expensive tickets to see her idols, the Spice Girls. They inspired her because they had come from a poor background like she had.

When she was 10, Adele's grandfather died of heart disease. She was so upset she decided to become a cardiac surgeon. She wanted to "fix people's hearts."[3] But everything changed at 14, when she was accepted to the BRIT School for Performing Arts.

At BRIT, students danced and practiced speeches in the halls. "As soon as I got a microphone in my hand," Adele said, "I realized I wanted to do this."[4]

When Adele was 15, she came across some jazz CDs in a sale bin. The music of Ella Fitzgerald and Etta James inspired her. Songs, she realized, could speak to people decades after they were recorded. Adele knew that was the kind of music she wanted to sing. She wanted to touch people's hearts.

Chapter 2

THE ROAD TO FAME

Eighteen-year-old Adele was furious with her boyfriend when she found out he was seeing someone else. Their argument in a London pub grew heated. When a security guard approached her, Adele turned and ran. She fled down the street with no idea where she was going. Even when the guard stopped, Adele kept running. As she looked down at the pavement, the title of her next song came to her. "Chasing Pavements" would be her first major hit.

Adele had written her first song when she was 16. She shut herself in her bedroom with her guitar. In ten minutes, she'd composed a simple tune called "Hometown Glory."

◄ **Adele poses at the 2011 MTV Video Music Awards.**

▲ **Adele performs at a jazz festival in Switzerland in 2008.**

"Hometown Glory" was one of three demo tracks that Adele completed for a school project and posted to social media. A record company executive heard the songs and was impressed. He signed Adele to a contract a few months after she graduated from high school.

Now Adele was expected to record a whole album, but she still had only three songs. For almost a year, she struggled with writer's block. "I was almost ready to give up," she said.[5]

"Chasing Pavements" was the breakthrough idea she needed. After that, new lyrics flowed freely. Adele called her album *19*, taking the title from her age when she began recording it.

Six months before the album was released, a nervous Adele appeared on British TV for the first time. She found herself on stage between Björk and Paul McCartney. She was so starstruck that afterward she couldn't stop crying.

In October of 2008, Adele appeared on *Saturday Night Live*. Within 24 hours, her debut album was the number one bestseller on iTunes.

Adele's mother loved her daughter's newest song. She reminded Adele of her childhood dream. "You *are* a surgeon," she said. "You're fixing people's hearts."[6]

"I feel relieved when I'm singing, whether I'm in the shower or cooking or onstage. I could sing forever. It's pure pleasure."[7]

—Adele

Chapter 3

THE SOUND OF SILENCE

In January of 2011, Adele had just set out on a world tour to promote her second album, *21*. She was on stage in Paris, France when suddenly her voice disappeared. "It was literally like someone pulled a curtain over it," she said.[8] Doctors diagnosed her with laryngitis and told her to rest. After a few weeks, she returned to singing. But it happened again in May. She lost her voice a third time while singing at her best friend's wedding in October. By now she knew something was seriously wrong.

"I cried a lot," Adele said. "But crying is really bad for your vocal cords, too!"[9]

◀ Adele's second album, *21*, was the
best-selling album of the year in 2011.

▲ **Adele chats with talk show host Jonathan Ross in 2011.**

Adele was terrified when she learned that she needed throat surgery. She was afraid her singing career was over.

For weeks, Adele waited in silence to learn whether the operation would restore her voice. Not only was it successful, but her vocal range gained four notes.

"Now I just feel really at peace," Adele said after her recovery. "And really proud of myself. I've never fully appreciated the things that I've achieved until now."[10]

"Even though my music is melancholy, there's also joy in that. I hope I do bring joy to people's lives, and not just sadness, but I think there's a comfort in it."[12]

—Adele

After five months out of the spotlight, Adele returned to the stage at the 2012 Grammy Awards. She belted "Rolling in the Deep," her voice as powerful and beautiful as ever. The crowd gave her a standing **ovation**. She won six Grammys that night, including Album of the Year for *21*. "Mum," she said in her acceptance speech, "Girl did good."[11]

Chapter 4

25 AND BEYOND

Adele took out a notebook and a pen. Before she began writing new lyrics, she always noted her age on the first page. After drawing a two and a five, she stopped. She could hardly believe that she was already twenty-five years old.

In November of 2015, Adele released her third album, *25*. "My last record was a break-up record," she said, "and if I had to label this one, I would call it a make-up record. Making up for lost time. Making up for everything I ever did and never did. *25* is about getting to know who I've become without realizing."[13]

Adele's life had changed in big and unexpected ways. On October 19, 2012, she gave birth to a son, Angelo.

◄ **Adele won the Academy Award for Best Original Song in 2013.**

▲ **Adele hugs a young fan at a concert in Birmingham, England in 2016.**

In 2013, she won an Academy Award for the song "Skyfall." In 2016, she signed the biggest record deal in history.

During her 2016 world tour to promote *25*, confetti rained down on fans. Each piece was printed with a lyric from her music. "Throw your soul through every open door," Adele urged her audience.[14]

"I want to evolve as an artist. There's so much music I don't know about yet. I want to go on the road with my friends who are artists. I want to go and see things as a fan again."[15]

—Adele

THINK ABOUT IT

- What makes a song stand the test of time? Do you think Adele's music will be admired by future generations?
- Why do people enjoy sad songs? Can a sad song make the listener feel uplifted?
- Adele's mother compared her work to a heart surgeon's. Do you agree with this comparison? Is an entertainer's work similar to a healer's?

GLOSSARY

album (AL-buhm): An album is a collection of songs on one record. Adele released her first album in 2008.

alumna (uh-LUHM-na): An alumna is a woman who has attended a certain school. Adele is an alumna of the BRIT School.

cardiac (KAR-dee-ak): Cardiac means pertaining to the heart. Adele dreamed of becoming a cardiac surgeon.

celebrities (suh-LEB-ruh-teez): Celebrities are famous people. Adele was often starstruck when meeting celebrities.

demo tracks (DEM-oh TRAKZ): Demo tracks are songs that are recorded to showcase an artist's ability. Adele's demo tracks got the attention of a record producer.

flat (FLAT): A flat is a British term for an apartment. Adele lived with her mother in a small flat.

laryngitis (lar-in-JYE-tiss): Laryngitis is an inflammation of the voice box. A person with laryngitis has difficulty talking.

ovation (oh-VAY-shuhn): An ovation is a show of enthusiastic support from the audience for a performer. A standing ovation means that the audience really liked the performance.

signed (SIYND): An artist who is signed by a record company has a contract to make an album. Adele signed with the first record executive who contacted her.

SOURCE NOTES

1. CBS. "2009 GRAMMY Awards: Adele Wins Best New Artist." *YouTube*. YouTube, 11 Feb. 2009. Web. 8 Sept. 2016.

2. Ibid.

3. Hattie Collins. "Adele Interview: World Exclusive First Interview in Three Years." *i-D*. i-D Magazine, 26 Nov. 2015. Web. 8 Sept. 2016.

4. Larry Sutton, ed. *Adele: 2016 World Tour*. New York: *PEOPLE Magazine*, 2016. Print. 31.

5. Ibid. 42.

6. Hattie Collins. "Adele Interview: World Exclusive First Interview in Three Years." *i-D*. i-D Magazine, 26 Nov. 2015. Web. 8 Sept. 2016.

7. Neil McCormick. "Adele: The One to Watch in 2008." *The Telegraph*. Telegraph Media Group Limited, 31 Jan. 2008. Web. 8 Sept. 2016.

8. Jonathan Van Meter. "Adele: One and Only." *Vogue*. Vogue, 12 Feb. 2012. Web. 8 Sept. 2016.

9. Ibid.

10. Ibid.

11. The Telegraph. "Girl Did Good: Adele Tribute to Mum at Grammy Awards." *YouTube*. YouTube, 13 Feb. 2012. Web. 8 Sept. 2016.

12. Sam Lansky. "Adele on Motherhood, Social Media and Breaking Records." *Time*. Time Inc., 21 Dec. 2015. Web. 8 Sept. 2016.

13. Daniel Kreps. "Adele Talks 'Make-Up' Album *25* in Emotional Open Letter." *Rolling Stone*. Rolling Stone, 21 Oct. 2015. Web. 8 Sept. 2016.

14. Kitty Empire. "Adele Live Review: Born for the Big Stage." *The Guardian*. Guardian News and Media Limited, 6 March 2016. Web. 8 Sept. 2016.

15. Jonathan Van Meter. "Adele: One and Only." *Vogue*. Vogue, 12 Feb. 2012. Web. 8 Sept. 2016.

TO LEARN MORE

Books

Bingham, Hettie. *Adele: The Golden Voice*. London, England: Wayland, 2014.

Gagne, Tammy. *Adele*. Hockessin, DE: Mitchell Lane, 2013.

McDowell, Pamela. *Adele*. New York, NY: AV2 by Weigl, 2014.

Web Sites

Visit our Web site for links about Adele:

childsworld.com/links

Note to Parents, Teachers, and Librarians: We routinely verify our Web links to make sure they are safe and active sites. So encourage your readers to check them out!

INDEX